I0589083

Also by Justin Grimbol

Drinking Until Morning

The Crud Masters

The Creek

Published by Grindhouse Press
POB 292644
Dayton, OH 45429
www.grindhousepress.com

The Party Lords
Grindhouse Press #020
ISBN-13: 978-0-9883484-8-6
ISBN-10: 0988348489
Copyright © 2013 by Justin Grimbol. All rights reserved.

Cover photograph courtesy of Dorothy Bhawl.
www.dorothybhawl.com
eolq.tumblr.com

Grindhouse logo and all related artwork copyright © 2013 by
Brandon Duncan.
www.corporatedemon.com

This book is a work of fiction.

No part of this book may be reproduced, stored in a retrieval
system, or transmitted by any means without the written
permission of the author or publisher.

For Kalish

THE
PARTY
LORDS

ONE

Teenagers were everywhere. There were so many of them. They acted so awkward, but cool at the same time. Even the nerds seemed cool to me.

"Teenagers are so gross," Vicki said.

Vicki was my girlfriend. She hated driving me to school. I was thirty-two years old and still in high school. She thought that was lame.

"I just don't get you," Vicki said. "I was tired of high school by the time I was sixteen. How can you stand this shit?"

"It's fun," I said.

"This isn't like college, baby. It's not cool to get more than one high school degree."

"I think it's pretty cool."

I got out of the car and walked around to her window to get a kiss.

"You're getting too old for this," she said.

"I'm young at heart," I said.

"Too bad your dick isn't young at heart," she said.

"What do you mean?"

"Your performance this morning was . . ." She gave me a thumbs down while making a farting noise with her mouth. A couple kids heard her and laughed.

"Sorry," I said. "I'm just not a morning person. I feel all calm and reflective in the morning. I feel like an ancient Chinese poet. I'm not horny like I am the rest of the day."

She laughed. "That's cute. Well, when you get home I'm going to sit on your face and you can recite some haikus to my asshole."

There was a geeky freshman girl standing behind us. She looked traumatized.

"What the fuck are you looking at?" Vicky said.

The girl ran off.

I walked into the school.

I couldn't get used to how much everything had changed. The teenagers were all so hip. When I was a kid we all dressed like we were on *Dawson's Creek*. It was lame and we all knew it, but we couldn't help ourselves. Things had changed. Purple jeans were normal now. Thuggy kids dressed skater. Skater kids dressed thug. Being artsy wasn't nerdy anymore. It was hip.

THE PARTY LORDS

I found my buddy standing by my locker. His name was Ta-Bone. Get it? Ta-Bone? Cause he likes ta bone chicks. He had only put it in a couple girls, but he came up with his nickname and somehow it stuck.

He was my only friend. No one else had gotten used to going to high school with a thirty-two year old man yet. But Ta-Bone was a chill-master. He thought it was cool I was over thirty.

"What's up, Buttcrack?" he said. "How are those old man boobs hanging?"

That was my nickname. Buttcrack. I got that nickname because my butt crack was always sticking out.

"Dude, what's with your hair man?" he said. "You look like Simon and Garfunkel."

"At least I don't look like a white R Kelly," I said.

"R Kelly? I'll take that as a compliment. That dude loves to fuck."

A girl opened the locker next to mine. The girl had an ass like a rhinoceros. It was a terrifying-looking thing. It made me want to fall down on my knees and pray for forgiveness.

She noticed me staring, put her jacket away, grabbed her books, and ran off. I kept staring at her ass, wishing I could shoot tractor beams out of my eyes.

"Dude," Ta-bone said. "What's your deal?"

"What? She's nice-looking. That butt makes me nervous and sweaty."

"You re-enrolled in high school. You are surrounded by the sweetest, youngest high school ass, and you're checking out the one chick in school that looks like a full

3

grown adult."

"She looks youngish."

"Does not. That girl looks older than the old-ass chick you're dating."

Ta-Bone pointed to a girl he thought was attractive.

"Now would you look at the butthole on that chick," he said. "Now that's the good stuff."

The girl noticed us talking about her and gave us a dirty look. We weren't very discreet. Ta-Bone smiled and winked at her. She rolled her eyes and her friends laughed.

Our first class was Sex Ed. It was the worst Sex Ed class ever. The teacher was old and looked like a beanbag chair. Her voice sounded soggy. She kept talking about all the basic reproductive crap we had already learned in biology class. I just wanted to see a condom get put on a banana. That's always a good time. She didn't even do that. She just showed a condom still in the wrapper and told us to read the instructions.

"It's not that hard," she said.

Ta-Bone kept asking where the clit was so he could see the diagram of the vagina. After the third time he asked, the teacher caught on to what he was doing. She got really mad and told him to see the principal.

"Does anybody have any other questions?" she asked.

I raised my hand.

"I heard smoking weed lowers your sperm count. If you smoke enough, could it be used as a sexual contraceptive?"

The class laughed. I felt proud. It was the first time I was able to get a class laughing since I re-enrolled.

"One more comment like that and you can join your buddy in the principal's office."

The teacher went on being really boring. While she lectured I noticed this kid sitting across from me. He kept sticking his hands down his sweatpants to scratch and fondle his cock and balls. He was a big kid. He looked like he had glandular problems. I imagined he was slimy down there.

He took his hand out of his pants and sniffed it. He caught me staring. I smiled at him politely. He held out his hand to me as if he wanted me to take a sniff.

"No thanks," I said.

I pretended to listen to the teacher's lecture on genitals. Scratch Master kept staring at me. There was only so much I could take. I had this old lady talking about semen and then this kid trying to get me to smell his ball sweat. Fuck.

I raised my hand and asked to go to the bathroom. The teacher told me to hurry up. I had no plans of coming back to class. That old thing wasn't going to notice. I don't think she even knew what was going on.

I found Ta-Bone drinking from a water fountain.

"What up, Buttcrack?" he said. "You get kicked out too?"

I nodded.

He gave me a hug. Ta-Bone loved to hug. He gave great hugs.

A couple girls walked by. Ta-Bone let go and stared at their butts as hard as he could.

"Look at that girl's butthole," he said.

I laughed. What a vile thing to say.

"I bet you've never seen a butthole," I told him.

"Dude, it's not 1995 or some shit. There's this thing called the internet. And there's this thing called internet porn. So, yeah, I've seen a butthole before."

"Good point. But if you like ass so much how come you don't like that chick that has the locker next to mine?"

"That girl has too much booty. I like a girl whose booty doesn't look that different than my own. My booty is fucking fine as hell."

He turned around and pulled down his pants. The boy was right. He did have a nice little butt. It was hard not to admire a butt like that.

"Mr. Maxwell!" a teacher called from the other end of the hall. "Pull your pants up."

It was Ms. Worpath.

"My name's Ta-Bone!" he said.

"Aren't you two supposed to be in class?"

She moved quickly. This lady could really chew your ear off. Neither of us was in the mood for a ten minute lecture.

"Mr. David, I would think that a student as old as you would be more responsible."

She was lecturing us from a distance. We couldn't let

her get too close. Once she was too close, we'd be screwed.

"Run for it!" I yelled.

I didn't know if she was actually chasing us. It didn't matter. We were having a good time pretending she was. We ran as fast as we could. We ran past Home Ec and Ta-Bone sneaked in quickly and stole a cookie this girl had just baked.

"This cookie's awful," Ta-Bone said.

"Fuck you," the girl said.

Ta-Bone spit the chewed up cookie on the floor.

The teacher saw us and we continued running.

We ran all the way down to the first floor, past the cafeteria, cut through a gym class and into the boys' locker room.

"That was a close call," I said.

We sat on the linoleum floor and caught our breath. At first we thought we were alone, but then we heard the showers turn on.

"Someone's here," I whispered.

Ta-Bone took out his cell phone. He put his finger up to his lips to shush me, and motioned for me to follow him. We crept up to the showers. Ta-Bone held his phone camera out like it was some super sophisticated James Bond spy tool, took a picture, and checked out who was in the shower. He got a picture of the kid's dong.

"I would recognize that massive wang anywhere," he said. "Ralph, that you?"

"Go away," the kid in the shower said.

It was Ralph, Ta-Bone's cousin. He was this short, grimy goblin who wore the same WrestleMania sweatpants every day. He had dandruff that looked like Frosted Flakes. His dick was big though. He had that much going for him. That was one impressive shlong. A meat wand like that could cast a mighty spell if used by the right wizard. But Ralph was no Harry Potter. He never hooked up with anyone. So that thing was basically just ornamental. And he needed to wash it. That thing was covered in all sorts of smegma.

We peeked in, hoping to find Ralph bathing for once. The water ran, but Ralph stood away from the stream. He still had his clothes on. His dick was out. He was trying to put it under the stream of hot water.

Ta-Bone grabbed him by his arm and dragged him out of the shower.

"Ta-Bone dude, wuzzz up?"

"What the fuck are you doing?" he asked.

"Oh, you know, sometimes I like to punish myself. It's no big deal."

"What do you mean?"

"I was going to make myself stand under burning hot water. But then the water was too hot and I didn't want to get fully naked, so I figured I would just punish my dick. But even that was too scary."

He stuck a finger up his nose and pulled out a crusty booger and stuck it in his mouth.

"What do you have to be upset about?" Ta-Bone asked.

"It was awful," Ralph said. "I didn't even want to go to school today. I'M A MONSTER!"

"What happened?" Ta-Bone asked.

"I was trying to teach myself how to bone chicks," he said. "I was using my pillow like you told me to."

"That's good," Ta-Bone said. "It's like a punching bag."

"I humped it forever. But I couldn't cum. I figured that coming would be like peeing, that I would just let it out, but it wasn't like peeing and . . ."

"Fuck dude, what happened?"

"I peed all over my pillow."

We tried to hold back our laughter, but it wasn't easy.

"It was awful. I felt like a rapist. I raped my pillow and then peed on it. I'm awful."

"I don't think fucking your pillow counts as actual rape," I said.

"You sure?"

"I mean its super weird. But no, it's fully legal."

He smiled. His mood had shifted drastically. "Hey, can you guys tell me if my armpits smell bad?"

He lifted his arm.

"Ralph, I'm telling you right now, that arm pit smells like a shit, for real," Ta-Bone said.

"It doesn't smell good," I said.

"But if it doesn't smell good, then why do I like smelling it so much?"

Mr. Phillips, the gym teacher, found us hiding out in the locker room. I had known Mr. Phillips for a while. We were in the same grade. We had never gotten along. One time, he caught me dry humping his sister, Candy. Actually, my good buddy Louie and I were both dry humping her at the same time. I had the butt side and he had the vagina side. It was surprisingly romantic. Candy liked dry humping. She said it was like "extreme hugging." Anyway, he caught us going to town and has had a vendetta against us ever since. I wouldn't have signed up for gym class, but I love tag so much.

"What are you slack jawed faggots doing here?" he said.

"We were just talking about exercise and shit," Ta-Bone said.

"Very funny. David, or Buttcrack, or Big Titties, or whatever it is you call yourself these days, can I speak with you alone?"

He told my friends to leave. At first they were hesitant. Mr. Phillips walked up to them and stared them down with crazy-abusive-dad eyes. Ralph and Ta-Bone ran off, leaving me alone with my nemesis.

"Sit," Mr. Phillips told me. He spoke to me like I was a dog.

There was nothing to sit on. I ended up sitting on the floor. He thought that was funny. His bald head seemed to get extra shiny when he was happy.

"I saw you talking to my niece," he said.

"You have a niece?"

I didn't know who he was talking about. I had not actually talked to any girls. High school girls didn't like me much. They thought I was creepy. I didn't want to tell him that though.

"If you do to her what you did to her mother, I just want you to know, I will have you arrested."

"Is dry humping teenagers illegal?"

"If you are a thirty-year-old man, yes."

"I don't know about that."

"Listen to me, I will have you arrested. Mark my words. I will have you arrested and then I will hire someone in prison to buttfuck you. He will buttfuck you so hard you will have a prolapsed anus and then he will suck on your prolapsed anus."

"Is that a thing?" I asked.

"Oh yeah, it's getting popular, you stunted, pitiful, useless, abomination of a man."

I smiled. It was a nervous, pitiful smile.

"Listen," he said. "The only reason they let you come back here at all is because your Grandma used to work here like a million years ago. Somehow that still carries clout. But I think it's pathetic. I think *you* are pathetic. I don't see how a full grown man can live his life this way."

He looked at me like he had just asked a question. I didn't know what to say.

"I'm sorry," I said.

"You're sorry?" he said.

"I guess."

He shook his head.

"Get out of here," he said.

Ta-Bone and Ralph were waiting for me outside the

locker room. Ralph was chewing on his hair.

"What happened in there?" Ta-Bone asked. "Did I hear him say he was going to buttfuck you?"

"No, he just wanted to chat about old times."

TWO

loved lunch at school. They served these french fries that had been sitting under a heat lamp for eternity. It tasted like carnival food.

I was lonely though. Ta-Bone didn't have the same lunch time as me. So I sat by myself.

As I was working on my second sack of french fries, a kid I liked to call Perfect Kid came near me. Perfect Kid was only fifteen but he looked older than I was. He wasn't balding like me or as rundown and droopy. But he was a giant, at least six-foot-four and he had these broad shoulders and a burly beard. He was a hippie. Hippie kids were not popular when I first went to high school. Perfect Kid was very popular.

His charm was undeniable. The boy made me feel like there was a chance for a world with no war, where all mankind loved each other. The kid was a pussy magnet.

Hell, he made me blush when he sat next to me.

"What's going on, man?" he asked.

"Not much."

"So you're old, right? Not that that's a bad thing. I once spent a very romantic night with a fifty-year-old woman in a ski lodge. She was very wise about life and love."

"I'm thirty," I told him.

"Awesome. So, anyway, I'm having a party tonight. It's going to be amazing. My house is big and in the middle of nowhere. I mean I have, like, NO neighbors. It's great."

"That's cool."

"Yeah, it is. But here's the thing. I look like an adult, but I don't have an ID. So I was wondering if you could pick us up some booze."

"Sure, I could do that."

"No shit?"

"I don't see why not. Am I invited to the party?"

"Of course."

I spent the rest of the day trying to find Ta-Bone. I was excited to tell him the good news. But he was nowhere to be found.

I was about to get on the bus and head home when I saw him drive a purple minivan onto the sidewalk.

"Where the hell did you get this thing?" I asked.

"It's my dad's old van. It's been all fucked up and broken and shit. I fixed this bitch up. Now it's looking sexy as hell. Admit it, just looking at this fine vehicle gives you a hard on. You got pre-jack soaking through your jeans right now."

"What was wrong with it?"

"Its headlights were all fucked up. But then I was like, fuck headlights. And I taped on a whole fuck load of flashlights. That's some creative shit, if you ask me."

I looked over and saw the broken headlight and the flashlights that had been sloppily taped to it. Other students were looking at us and snickering. I liked the attention. They were laughing at us, but deep down they knew this vehicle was badass in an apocalyptic, Mad Max: Road Warrior sort of way.

"Hey! Get that van off the sidewalk."

I looked over. Mrs. Worpath was after us again. I jumped into the front window of the van. Ralph tried to pull me in. Ta-Bone peeled away with my legs still dangling out the window.

We drove to a cul-de-sac and smoked a joint. It was our favorite spot. There was nothing there but quickly built mansions that hadn't been moved into yet. It was peaceful. The homes seemed young, clean, sturdy. Usually when I looked at people's homes I imagined families eating home cooked meals and then watching sitcoms together and it made me feel homesick. Or I thought about families fighting and ignoring each other and, strangely, that made me feel homesick too. These homes were different. They were empty. I liked that.

I waited until we were stoned to tell them the news.

Ta-Bone had that proud dad look on his face. Ralph looked shocked.

"Man, I don't know why we haven't done this before. I always figured that they revoked your booze buying privileges when you re-enrolled in high school."

"No, I can still buy booze."

"Now, you aren't fucking with me? We got invited to one of Perfect Kid's parties?"

"We really did."

"I've never been invited to a party before," Ralph said.

"This is going to be wild as hell," Ta-Bone said. "I'm going to bone so much mushy poon tonight. I bet each one of us will fall in love. For real, this night is going to be romantic. It's going to rain pussy sauce."

He danced around the van. Well, it wasn't so much dancing as he just sort of dry humped the air. Ralph and I joined him. Soon we were all gangbanging the cool fall breeze, feeling perfect.

We decided that we were too amped up. So we smoked another bowl and got a little too stoned.

At one point I saw someone wandering through the woods. It looked like Crotch Sniffer. He looked like he was watching us.

I pointed him out to Ta-Bone and Ralph.

Ralph waved to him.

"Don't wave," I said.

"I bet he's just hunting some shit," Ta-Bone said.

"He doesn't have guns."

THE PARTY LORDS

"This is the most boring conversation I have ever had," Ta-Bone said. "Who cares what that redneck is doing in the woods, just let him be."

THREE

I once owned a Gibbous Peak Monopoly. All the businesses in town put it together. It was awesome. The Cigar Bar was Boardwalk. Cozy Video was Park Place, though it went out of business right before the game came out. It was now this weird shop where a bony lady sold crystals and books on astrology. Conca's Pizza was Baltic, which I thought was bullshit cause Baltic was the lamest property and Conca's was the best restaurant in town. It always seemed unjust to me. The water utility was the Bonnie's Liquor Store. I loved that. Bonnie's Liquors seemed just as vital as water at times. There were other liquor stores in town, but Bonnie's was the only one with forties. Gibbous Peak was too fancy for forties. They didn't even have forties at the 7-11. Bonnie's seemed like it had every kind of booze you could imagine. It was like Willy Wonka's booze factory. So this is where I went to buy the alcohol for Perfect Kid's party. By the time I was done shopping, I had an entire shopping cart full of booze. The lady at the register did not look impressed.

"I'm going to need to see your I.D.," she said.

She had sold me booze countless times, but she was still carding me.

I reached into my pocket and my heart sank. My wallet was gone. I still had the cash Perfect Guy gave me, but I couldn't find my wallet.

The lady could tell what was going on. She looked pissed.

"Look, I'm obviously old as hell," I told her.

"Store policy says I am going to have to see some sort of identification."

"I just can't find my wallet. Can I leave this booze here and come back for it?"

She looked me over.

"I guess. Hurry up though."

My young friends weren't nearly as panicked as I was. They had never lost a wallet before. They didn't understand the kind of hassle it could be to get things back.

"Let's just go looking for it," Ta-Bone said.

I drove back to school. It wasn't there. We searched all over the perimeter of the building. Nothing.

Eventually I tried to go to a couple more liquor stores, hoping they wouldn't ID me. Ta-Bone said I looked old as shit, that it was a fluke I got ID'd at all.

Each liquor store we went to ID'd me.

There was one more place to check.

FOUR

"Where are we going now?" Ralph asked.

"My place."

"I can't wait to see your movie collection," Ralph said. "I bet you have, like, every *Rocky* movie ever made."

"What makes you think I have a movie collection?"

"Just figured."

"I did once. But I had to sell it to pay the rent."

He looked confused. What I told him was incomprehensible. It was as outlandish as getting attacked by a shark or being abducted by aliens. For me it was all too real. I felt old.

I pulled up to my apartment building and took ten deep breaths.

"You guys should wait here," I said.

"Why?" Ta-Bone said. "I want to see the smoking hot

old chick you've been blasting away on."

"Trust me, just stay here."

I walked up to my apartment building and buzzed our door. I couldn't pay my share of the rent, so Vicky took my keys away. She didn't care if I slept there, but she didn't think it was fair that I had all the privileges she had. Plus, she said this would give me incentive to find a job. I told her I had a job. I was a student. That didn't go over well.

"Who is it?" her voice sounded eerie and seductive over the speaker. I always enjoyed the way voices sounded over intercoms. They're all cracky and hoarse and sexy-sounding.

"It's Buttcrack."

"Who?"

"I mean David."

"Hey baby! You ready for a rematch?"

"I guess so."

She buzzed me in. The sound gave me goose bumps. It was like Freddy Krueger running his blades. I walked up the stairs slowly. I didn't want to hook up, so I walked super slowly, hoping she would be out of the mood by the time I got there.

I couldn't escape her mighty poon. As soon as I stepped into that apartment, I had such a hard on. My dong didn't have a chance.

"Hey baby," I said. "You seen my wallet?"

"No baby."

"Fuck, I lost my wallet and . . ."

"Forget your wallet," she said.

She bent over the kitchen counter. That was all it took. I fell to my knees, lifted up her skirt, spread open her ass and looked at that rugged asshole and then started tonguing it. She had a very sensitive anus. I almost got her to come that way but she grabbed me and pulled me up and then I put it in her vagina area.

I heard someone laughing. It came from the window. I looked over and saw Ta-Bone and Ralph looking in. How the fuck did they get up there? I looked at them and they both laughed their asses off. I motioned for them to leave. They just laughed harder. I didn't want to let Vicki catch on so I started fucking her as hard and as deeply as I could.

"Oh Davey, you have never dug into me like this before!" she moaned. "Now go down there and lick my tiny little anus again."

"I'd rather stay up here," I said.

"Come on, you love my poop hole!"

"I'm just really loving your vagina right now!"

I looked at the window.

Ralph stuck his tongue out, then lifted his shirt up and pressed his nipples against the window.

"Oh Davey," Vicky moaned. "You've never fucked me like this! I've never been so turned on."

She came hard and then pulled away. I felt dizzy.

She bent me over the counter. "Now it's your turn, big boy."

She pulled the turkey baster out of the oven and put it

in my mouth.

"Suck it, like it's a sweaty man cock," she said. "Come on, suck it."

I had no idea how she couldn't hear Ta-Bone and Ralph laughing, but she was acting completely oblivious.

"Come on!" she yelled. "Really slobber on it!"

I sucked the turkey baster.

"Be gentle," I said.

"Let's think of this as you paying your rent."

I hocked a big juicy loogey on the counter. It looked like a dead jellyfish. Vicki sucked it into the turkey baster.

"Now remember," she said. "The trick to relaxing the sphincter is to push out."

"I know, I know!"

"Don't be so impatient," she said.

She pushed the thing against my butthole. The pressure was intense. I took a breath before pushing out. It slid in. It burned for a moment then felt pleasant, then burned again. She moved it in and out slowly. She reached around and jerked my dick. Ta-Bone and Ralph stopped laughing.

I loved getting reamed out by the turkey baster. But I didn't want to traumatize my buddies. The turkey baster made me feel old. I wanted to look back at the window, but I couldn't bear seeing their faces.

Vicki squeezed the handle. Phlegm shot into my rectum.

I came.

I came hard.

And then I needed to shit. Getting fucked by the turkey baster always made me need to shit. It left no time for cuddling. I ran to the bathroom with come still dripping out of my dong.

"You okay, hon?" Vicky asked as I stumbled out of the bathroom. "I gave it to you kinda hard in there."

At that moment, I felt like I could ask her anything. Taking a turkey baster up the ass entitled me to a favor or two. So I told her about my predicament.

"I'm sorry, honey, but I just cleaned this entire apartment and I haven't seen your wallet."

"Fuck, well, then maybe, just maybe, do you think, you could maybe buy the beer?"

"Are you out of your mind?" she said.

"Baby, I just need your help."

"This is bullshit. I mean, this is getting really pathetic."

"I'm just . . ."

"You want me to go and buy beer for a bunch of teenagers—something that is highly illegal—just so you can chill with the cool kids?"

"It's not *that* illegal."

"You know what? You can go off and play teenager, but don't expect me to get involved. I'm a fully grown woman. I got a job that I love."

"You wait tables at the same place you've been working since you were sixteen."

She didn't like that.

"I think you should find somewhere else to sleep tonight."

I tried to apologize but she refused to even speak to me. All she did was point to the door and stare at me with eyes that made my heart feel sorer than my butt-hole.

I expected Ta-Bone and Ralphy to be traumatized by what they had seen, but they didn't even seem upset. They were laughing. As soon as Ta-Bone saw me, he ran up to me and gave me a big hug.

"That was the most badass thing I've ever seen!" he said. "Are you okay?"

"Yeah, I'm fine."

"You old dudes are fucked up," he said.

"I'm sorry you all had to see that," I said.

"Don't be. For real, that was the gnarliest, most fucked up and hilarious thing I've ever seen. Doesn't it hurt to take it up the ass?"

"It stings. But it also feels good."

"Have you ever taken dick up the ass?" Ta-Bone asked.

"No, just a turkey baster. Well, and a dildo and a sharpie, and some other random stuff."

"A dildo is basically a dick."

"Well, there was no man at the other end of it."

"I once put my finger in a dog's butt," Ralph said. "It bit me. That was the last time I did that. Well, it was almost the last time."

He smelled his finger as if it might still smell like dog butt.

Ta-Bone ignored his cousin. He put his hand on my shoulder. "Your GF going to buy us some booze?"

"No, she's mad at me right now."

"How mad?"

"Super mad."

"Bitch is crazy. You just took a turkey baster in the ass. It takes a special kinda motherfucker to do some shit like that. Girl should buy you whatever you want whenever you want."

"Yeah, well, it doesn't really work that way."

"I don't get it," he said.

"Let's just get out of here."

It was dark. We were going to have to turn on the flashlights.

FIVE

They got hungry. We searched the minivan for change. We found fifteen bucks. We were stunned. We took our pile of change to Conca's to get some pizza. I passed a cop on the way over to the place and he didn't pull me over. Maybe the flashlights really did effectively double as a headlight.

We ate our pizza slowly. Ralph had taken all the cheese off his and made a giant cheese ball. He didn't seem to want to eat it. He was proud of his sculpture. But eventually he got too hungry and he ate it.

I noticed a couple strange dudes ordering pizza. They looked messed up. They had small heads and their eyes were like chunks of gravel. Their hands were massive and they were dirty. Too dirty.

The angry pizza shop guys didn't like them much.

"I told you two you weren't allowed in here," one of the guys yelled. "Leave before I call the cops."

The dirty guys made grunting noises and then left.

I had been living in that town all my life. It's not that big. Maybe six thousand people lived there. I had never seen so many run down, messed up, grimy-looking characters. There was the recession, but it felt like there had always been a recession. Who were these people? First there was the crotch sniffer, and now these dudes.

"Damn," Ta-Bone said. "Did you see those guys? Ralph, they were even dirtier than your ass."

"The McMurtrys," he said. His voice sounded deep, like he was telling a ghost story.

"Who the fuck are the McMurtrys?" I asked.

"They're a family that lives deep, deep in the woods," Ralph went on. "They wear dead squirrels for condoms. They put rocks in their buttholes. I have proof. Our cousin Betty fucked one once. She still has one of the rocks."

"It's true," Ta-Bone said, using the same deep tone.

"I find this all hard to believe."

"They're all inbred," Ta-Bone said.

"Yeah," Ralph said. "And they eat people's butts, kinda like you did, but they don't just lick it, they chew it and swallow the whole butt. THE WHOLE BUTT!"

"How come I've never seen them before?" I asked.

"Shit, I don't know," Ta-Bone said. "You're kinda clueless."

We were about to order another round of slices when this

woman walked in. She had a massive ass. It could barely fit in her skintight khakis.

"Oh shit! Look at that ladies butthole," Ta-Bone said. "I bet she has two buttholes. Maybe three."

The woman turned around. At first she looked deeply offended and ready to rip us apart.

Then she saw me.

"David?"

"Annie Duma?"

"Oh my God! I haven't seen you in years! What brought you back to town?"

"I still live here."

Her family walked in. She introduced me to her husband. He shook my hand so hard I almost cried mercy. Their kids wore matching polo shirts. They also had strong grips.

"Why don't you all join us? I'll buy us a big pie of pizza," she said.

"No, we've already had a slice."

Ta-Bone nudged me with his elbow to remind me of our mission at hand. Annie could probably get us booze. I had to get her away from her day laborer husband, but once I managed that, it would be easy. She had always been a pushover.

I smiled politely. "I would love to have dinner with you."

Annie had a good life. Her husband, Mike, had a landscaping business. It was doing well. They kept taking on new clients. Her kids did well in school. They had just got back from Foxwoods casino and had won five grand. They were going to be going on a cruise later in the month. "We're so blessed," she kept saying.

"And how have you been?" she asked.

"Been good," I said. "Busy."

Busy. Grownups loved that word. I knew I would sound more grownup if I said I was busy.

Annie smiled. "Mike, David and I used to have so much fun together. David used to be so crazy."

"You two dated?" Mike asked.

"No," she said. "Well, there was this one time. You know what we used to call him? Mr. Cop-a-cheapy-while-you-sleepy. Seriously, every time you slept at this kid's house, you'd wake up with him feeling you up. I mean, he never, like, really molested anyone. But he would just cuddle in a really creepy way."

Her kids didn't seem interested in the story their mom was telling. If my mom told a story like that, I would have been really freaked out. These kids must have been used to their mom saying tactless shit.

"Mr. Cop-a-cheapy-while-you-sleepy?" Ta-Bone said. "That nickname's long as fuck, but it kinda works. We call him Buttcrack."

She looked suspicious of Ta-Bone and Ralph. I think she knew they were too old to be my kids.

"So are you babysitting or . . .?"

Ta-Bone laughed. "A babysitter? Shit, I was born too old for a babysitter."

"Then how do you know each other?"

"We all go to high school together."

Annie looked confused. I explained how I had re-enrolled in high school.

"That's interesting. Are you going to graduate soon and then go to college?"

"I don't plan on it," I said.

"How do you make money?"

"He sells his DVDs," Ralph said.

"Buttcrack is the man," Ta-Bone said. "We just saw him wailing away on a smoking hot piece of ass and then take it up the butt with a turkey baster."

"You did? Well, isn't that nice," Annie said.

The two little boys looked at each other and laughed.

"Was it a high school girl?" Mike asked. "I bet you like that young stuff don't you?"

"Mike, stop," Annie said.

"It's an honest question."

"It's not appropriate."

"Oh, what, and the story you just told was?"

"High school girls are too young to be having sex," Annie said.

"Are not."

"Would you want our children having sex?"

The two boys gave each other sleazy smiles. These two demons knew what fucking was. They were only four or five, but they didn't seem to be the type of kids that believed in the tooth fairy. And if they did, they would probably fantasize about date raping her.

"Baby," Mike said, "I lost my virginity when I was ten years old. So . . ."

"No you didn't."

"Did too. And it was with my fifteen-year-old cousin."

"No way," Ta-Bone said. "That's possibly the coolest thing I have ever heard. Holy shit, you've been banging beaver since you were ten?"

"My cousin, Lenny, and me had a pee fight once," Ralph said.

"Shut up, Ralph. I want to hear more about Mike banging out when he was ten."

Mike held up his pinky. "My dick was this big," he said. "It was this big. I put it in her though. I didn't know what the hell I was doing."

"That's so gross," Annie said.

"I think it's awesome," Ta-Bone said. "Don't you agree, Buttcrack?"

"It is kinda awesome."

"I was just a kid," Mike continued. "I didn't know any better. It was no big deal."

Annie looked outraged. "I think it's sick."

"It is not," Mike said. "You're just being a bitch right now."

"Ten-year-olds are not supposed to have sex. Especially with their cousins. Why are you so gross? You're a pedophile."

There was a woman with her two kids sitting at the table next to ours. She got tense when she heard Annie call her husband a pedophile. Her kids also looked upset. They were not as desensitized as Annie's kids.

"You're a fucking child molester!" Annie yelled.

"Am not."

"You fucked a fifteen-year-old girl."

"I was ten."

"I don't care what your excuse is."

The pizza guys had started laughing. The woman and her children got up and left. Annie rolled her eyes.

They went back and forth like this for a while. We watched. It was scary, but also extremely entertaining. Eventually Annie really lost her shit. She started banging her fists on the table, screaming about how she hated being married to Mike and that she was never going to sleep with him again.

"Ask her," Ta-Bone said.

"I don't think now is a good time," I told him.

"Just do it."

Annie overheard us.

"What do you need to ask me?" she asked.

"Nothing," I said. "It's not important."

"No, ask," she said. "I want to know."

"I lost my wallet and my ID and I was wondering if you could buy us beer."

"Are you fucking kidding me?"

Mike smiled. He knew I had taken the attention off him and put it on myself. Pretty soon she was going to start calling me a pedophile.

"This is so inappropriate," she said. "You need to grow up, David."

"I should go."

"You've always been a bit stunted, but you should at least be out of high school by now."

I got up, kissed her on the cheek and said goodbye.

"Bye, David."

"Keep nailing those high school chicks!" Mike said.
"You're such an ass," Annie said.
And their fight continued.

SIX

After my run-in with Annie and her brood, I wanted nothing to do with people my own age. But Ta-Bone convinced me that reconnecting with old friends was the only way to get booze.

"You gotta call up other old people," he said. "Straight up, that is the only way we're getting any booze."

He had a point. We sat in the parking lot of 7-11 and thought about who I might call that wouldn't be a complete torture chamber to spend time with. Most of my old friends didn't live in the area anymore.

"I could call my buddy Chris," I said. "He used to be a party animal. But he's a cop now."

"You gotta know somebody who's, like, a complete drunk," Ta-Bone said.

I knew who I needed to call. His name was Lewis. He

was easily the sloppiest wreck of a man I knew. I called up my old buddy. He was happy to hear from me. He gave me his address and told me to come over.

While we were driving, I told the kids about Lewis's exploits. I wasn't trying to hype him up or make the kids laugh. I wanted to warn them. Lewis liked to party a little too hard. It could get disturbing.

But it didn't work. They looked excited, like they were going to meet a celebrity.

We pulled up to Lewis's place. I figured Lewis probably lived in the basement so I called him up, not wanting to wake up the family that lived upstairs. I could see kids' toys stacked in the windows. I felt bad for whatever little boy or girl lived above Lewis. They would grow up having to listen to the worst metal and the creepiest sex noises a person could imagine.

"You here?" Lewis asked when he answered the phone.

"Yeah, how do we get in?"

"What do you mean?"

The phone hung up and the front door opened. Lewis stood there. He was dressed strangely. He kinda looked like a white Bill Cosby.

I walked up and he gave me a hug.

"Hey buddy, how's it going?" he said.

Back in the day, he would have called me a cocksucker or fat ass. Now he was calling me buddy. It felt wrong.

And this was his home. Lewis owned the whole thing. I couldn't believe it. At first I thought he must have won the lottery, or that maybe his parents had died and he had inherited money. But that was not the case. He had a job. He had started his own taxi service. He had actual furniture and it didn't look like it was bought at a thrift store. It looked nice . . . quaint.

My friends seemed eager to hear tales of his partying. But he had none. His wife and he had a child. It was the biggest, drooliest baby I had ever seen. It acted more like the Lewis I once knew.

It was nice though. The stories about raising his son were unbelievably boring, but I enjoyed every second. I enjoyed seeing my friend being a father and laughing every time his baby burped.

"Have you talked to Craig at all?" he asked.

"No," I said.

"Really," he said. "You two were like best buds."

"Who's Craig?" Ralph asked.

"You haven't told your . . ." He realized he didn't know who these random teenagers were. "Are they your cousins?"

I told him about how I re-enrolled in high school. He didn't seem shocked. "Hey man, we all have our own pace. It's not like you have a kid or something. Wait, do you?"

"No. I don't have a kid."

"I'm telling you it's the best, man. It's life changing. It makes you feel all 'oh shit, I have a kid, I got to like, pay for lots of shit, I better work a lot.' It's wild."

"I imagine."

"Do you have more hot chocolate?" Ralph asked.

"Yeah, go in the kitchen. Help yourself. We got tons of snacks. Make yourself at home."

"Thanks, man."

"No problem."

Ralph walked into the kitchen.

"Nice kid. So you two are just like, pals?"

"Sorta."

"That's cool, I guess."

"So where's your wife?" I asked.

"Honey!" he called out. "Come out and meet my buddy."

Lewis's wife came out. She was a good-looking woman. She had short red hair, and big breast-feeding boobies.

"Hi, I'm Lisa," she said.

Up until then, Ta-Bone had acted reasonably polite. This all changed once wifey came in. I could tell by the look in his eyes that he was going to freak out and start saying all sorts of dumb shit.

Please don't say the word butthole! I prayed.

"Damn!" Ta-Bone said. "Look at you. Buttcrack, you and Lewis ever dry hump that thing?"

Lewis's eyes widened. He looked at me and shook his head.

His wife looked flabbergasted. "What's going on? You humped something? Who's Buttcrack?" she asked.

I raised my hand slowly.

Her pouty eyes were like daggers. I felt awful.

"Honey, I honestly don't know what he's talking

about," Lewis said.

"He was just joking," I said.

"Chill out," Ta-Bone went on. "I'm sure this lady knows her husband's a crazed party animal. I'm sure he's told her about all the dry humping. It's no big deal. Everyone dry humps. You telling me you never dry humped? Husbands and wives don't keep secrets. I'm sure she knows about the piss fights and how you two used to shoot beer into each other's asses with turkey basters."

"That's . . . so . . . gross," she said.

Her voice was so soft and hurt-sounding. I could barely understand what she was saying.

"I know, the turkey baster thing is a little wild for me. I don't know what's up with that shit. I just figured that's some shit everyone did in the Nineties."

She looked away. "Lewis, baby . . ."

"I don't know what the hell's going on," he said. "I . . ."

She looked at me. "Is all that true?"

I was bad at lying. If I was ever captured in war I would give away every secret I knew as soon as the enemy looked at me the wrong way.

"It was just one time," I said. "We didn't do it all the time. I . . ."

"David, what have you been telling these kids?" Lewis asked.

"Buttcrack told us all kinds of good shit," Ta-Bone said. "He told us you used to poo in swimming pools and pee on dogs. He told us you used to use cocaine while sitting on the toilet, cause it gave you diarrhea."

"You used to do cocaine?" she said. "Is this all true?"

Ta-Bone went on. "He told us that you used to dance all crazy. He told us you used to dance even when there was no music playing."

"Dear god, Ta-Bone," I said. "Shut the fuck up!"

"What's your problem?" he said.

"I think I need a glass of water," Lewis's wife said.

She walked to the kitchen.

I looked up at Lewis. He didn't look angry. Just embarrassed. I wished we could have brawled like we used to. We used to get drunk and fight all the time. But we weren't drunk. All we had was hot chocolate.

"Why would you tell people about all that stuff?" he said.

"I don't know," I said.

His wife screamed.

"Honey! Are you alright?"

She came back.

There were tears in her eyes.

Ralph stood beside her.

"What's going on?" Lewis asked.

"There's pubic hair all over our kitchen sink. This kid, this dirty little boy, put pubic hair everywhere."

"I was just joking around," he said. "Buttcrack told us Lewis used to put pubic hair in people's sink all the time. I thought you'd think it was funny."

"You pubed my sink?" Lewis asked.

"I pubed it good. You got to see it."

Now Lewis looked angry.

I grabbed Ta-Bone and Ralph and led them out of the

house. Ta-Bone acted confused. He couldn't understand why everyone was mad.

He blocked me from getting in the van.

"Why didn't you ask him to get us beer?" he asked.

"Are you serious?"

"Dude, you pussed out so bad back there."

"Are you delusional?" I said. "Did you see how embarrassed he was?"

"I don't know man. You old motherfuckers get embarrassed about everything. We were just reminding him of how badass he used to be. Not that I feel bad for the guy. His baby is fucked up-looking but did you see the butthole his wife had?"

"No, I didn't see her butthole. I saw how happy they were, until you had to bring up all the secrets I had told you."

"You didn't say they were secrets."

"I figured it was obvious. God, I feel like I'm fucking babysitting you guys."

I heard my phone beep. There was a text from Lewis.

"Dude WTF?"

I texted back that I was sorry.

"Get out of my driveway. Wife is pissed," he wrote back.

SEVEN

I kept thinking about Lewis's life and how cozy it must be. I felt homesick. Not for my home. I didn't feel homesick for Vicki and her turkey baster (no matter how hard that thing made me cum), or my parents' place. I felt homesick for everyone's cozy-looking home I drove by. Fall was ending. It was just starting to get cold. Everyone looked cozy. I wanted to be adopted by some random family.

I noticed Ta-Bone had my cell phone.

"What are you doing?"

"Looking for someone that could buy us beer. You don't have many friends. I have so many more numbers in my phone."

"I'm sure you do. Now give me that."

"Who are you going to call?" Ralph asked.

I didn't want to call anyone. But it looked like Ta-

THE PARTY LORDS

Bone had already texted my buddies Craig and Troy. Troy texted back immediately, saying I should come over.

Troy was a rich kid. He spent his summers traveling in India and Morocco. He smoked a lot of weed. And partied. Chicks loved this guy. But his mind was all over the place. Some weeks he acted like a studly monk, like he was trying to become a weird cult leader. Other weeks he would act like he wanted to become a professional party animal. He studied books on mixology and the history of whisky. He sold drugs for a while. Sometimes his spiritual phases and his party phases would overlap. One time I went to his house to buy mushrooms and I found him meditating in the basement. I had to wait three hours for him to stop. He just sat there for three hours getting all peaceful in his mind and shit. And then he sold me some Xanax.

The only problem was that he lived in the Hill, a weird beehive of houses on the far end of town. I rarely went there. It's easy to get lost in the Hill. Too easy. Kids loved to go up there for Halloween. I hated Halloween in the Hill. I always got separated from my friends. I felt tense as soon as I entered the Hill. And, of course, as I expected, I got lost instantly.

I was getting really irritated. Ta-Bone and Ralph didn't give a shit about being lost.

The flashlights didn't help much. I had to drive slowly.

"Maybe we should just give up on the whole beer buying thing," Ralph suggested. "Maybe we should have a sober party. We could take a bath in my pool. Baths are more fun with other people. Plus I'm starting to stink."

"Damn, Ralph," Ta-Bone yelled. "Did you just say 'sober party'? That just made my skin crawl. Fuck. And I know that you don't have an actual pool. You have a kiddy pool. That shit is filled with leaves and dead chipmunks and shit."

"We're fine," I said. "I'm sure my buddy Troy can help out. He's chill."

"Your other friends were not chill," Ralph said.

"They were fine," I said. "They were just doing their super adult thing."

A truck drove up behind us. It rode my ass hard. I sped up. It continued riding me. Headlights filled the van, blinding me.

"What the fuck is this guy's problem?"

Ta-Bone stuck his hand out the window and gave him the finger. I hit him in the stomach and told him to stop.

The truck pulled alongside us. The guy in the passenger side smiled at me. He looked messed up. His face looked waterlogged. He snorted at us. The driver leaned over. He had a face like a chicken. He sneered, showing us his tiny pointy teeth. They looked like the Crotch Sniffer and the guys that got kicked out of the pizza place, only ten times as ugly and sinister-looking.

They sped up again and pulled in front of us. A man stood in the back, naked, pissing. Urine splattered on my car's window. I tried to turn on the windshield wipers, but they didn't work. The piss kept coming. I swerved off the road.

The truck drove off.

I asked if everyone was ok. They all nodded. I stayed put and tried to calm down.

We stayed in the van with the doors locked. A car passed and we all flinched. We thought they had come back. Ralph started to cry. I reached back and held his hand. It was small and sweaty.

"I think we should go home," Ralph said. "We almost got Texas Chainsaw Massacred."

"I think I've been butt-raped enough for today," I said.

"Buttcrack, you're basically an Olympic athlete when it comes to assplay."

Usually, I felt proud of my assy adventures. But I felt a little uneasy about the kids knowing about them. Ta-Bone couldn't keep his mouth shut. By Monday the whole school would know that I take it in the rear.

I've always felt irresponsible, but that night I had brought it to a new level. I had introduced teenagers to assplay and, while trying to buy them alcohol, had gotten them attacked by inbreds.

"Maybe Ralph's right," I said. "Maybe we should call it a night."

"No, we got to get that beer," Ta-Bone said. "It's like a real life mission. I bet that goofy-looking chick with the big ass will be there."

A pair of headlights appeared in the distance. I thought it was the mutants.

Ralph started weeping again. "They're going to eat our buttholes to death!" he yelled.

"Oh fuck! Oh fuck! Oh fuck!" I kept saying.

I noticed the vehicle wasn't a truck but a Prius. Still, I didn't calm down. All I could think was, "Why are these inbred mutant rapists driving around in a Prius?"

Troy stuck his head out the window of the Prius. He looked at me and gave me a smile. Troy was the original perfect guy. When he smiled it was like the beginning of *The Lion King* when Simba is born and all the animals are singing.

"David, is that you?"

"Hey, Troy."

"I figured you got lost. I just had a feeling you needed my help."

"I got a little lost," I admitted.

"Well, follow me. My wife, Cassandra, is making some tea. It will help calm your soul."

We got in the van and followed them down the dark road.

Their home was like a shrine to everything New Age-y. Indian music played in the background. Buddha statues sat on every surface. The walls were covered in massive pictures of Cassandra meditating and doing yoga on the beach. She was nude in many of the pictures. The incense smoke was so thick it made me cough. I noticed Troy had a bindi on his forehead. So did Cassandra. Their kids were surprisingly calm. They looked hypnotized.

I asked Troy if he knew about the McMurtrys.

"Sure, why?"

"They tried to drive us off the road."

"Did you piss them off some way?"

"I don't think so."

"Maybe there's something poisonous about your aura," he said.

"I guess so. They look kinda crazy."

"They probably eat too much processed food."

"I think they're inbred."

"I'm sure the food they eat has something to do with it. You definitely need to eat better. You look like shit."

Troy noticed I was a little hurt. He gave me a big hug and asked me how I was doing.

"I'm okay."

"You don't look bad really. You look . . . you look the same as always."

"Yeah, except I'm balding."

"I have a tincture for that."

"I don't know what that is. Would it hurt?"

He laughed.

Cassandra came out and introduced herself. She didn't seem particularly thrilled to meet us but she gave us a hug and kiss.

Her hair was long and reached all the way down to her tiny butt. She had really intense cheekbones. She was in her pajamas, but she looked more dressed up than any girl I had ever dated.

We sat in their living room and drank tea. Cassandra told us about yoga school. Troy then told us about how he was writing about how aligning the chakras can help you make money.

"We are so grateful for all the support that has been uplifting and inspiring us in life," she said. "Our journey has been so blessed. I feel such ETERNAL LOVE!"

"It has been such an honor and blessing to share our knowledge and wisdom with the world," Troy said.

"It's just so important to really realize that realization is our destiny. You must ascend to the next dimension of receptivity and align with your highest self. You must penetrate through the boundaries of illusion and bask in the beauty of infinite light and expansive possibilities. Be humble, be grace, be truth, be song, be one."

"I'm into yoga," Ta-Bone said. He spoke in this soft voice I had never heard him use before. "I find it very healing. Very, umm, blessed. And it's so good for your body. I mean look at you. You look so flexible."

It was true. Cassandra was the longest, most flexible-looking woman I had ever seen. She looked like a Buddhist version of Spiderman with boobs.

They continued talking about their spiritual journey and all the money they had made. They felt like it was a gift from the spirits.

Ta-Bone asked her to do some yoga moves. She got on the floor and started stretching around. Soon she was doing headstands. It was like the moves cheerleaders do, but in slow motion.

Ralph's cell phone rang.

"God, Mom. I wear what I want. Stop being such a nerd. I'm trying to get laid by chicks tonight. Lots of chicks. God. Yeah I'm with an adult. Here, you can talk to him."

He passed me the phone.

"Hello."

Cassandra looked creeped out. I think she had just realized how young my friends were.

"Yeah, your son's with me. We're just watching movies and . . ."

"We don't allow movies in our house," Cassandra called out.

I shushed her. She didn't like that. The look in her eyes was intense. It made me nervous.

I handed the phone back to Ralph and tried to ignore the hateful look she was giving me. It wasn't easy.

"Hey Buttcrack, you should try this yoga thing out," Ta-Bone said.

"No, I'm okay," I said.

"So what have you been up to?" Troy asked me.

"I've been going to school and . . ."

"No, I mean, what have you been up to in here?" he motioned to the center of his chest. "I want to know how your spirit is doing."

"Eh, it's been decent, I guess. It depends if I'm getting laid or not," I said, trying a bit too hard to be funny.

No one laughed.

"I heard you had a girlfriend," Troy said.

"I do. I was talking about her. Kinda."

"Pig," Cassandra said under her breath.

Ta-Bone was doing yoga on his own now. He had twisted himself into some crazy-looking positions.

I asked how their kids were.

"Very centered," Cassandra said. "Why?"

"I was just wondering."

"I had them right here in my living room. No pain killers!"

She was yelling at me. I couldn't understand why.

"Are you ok?" I asked.

"Can I talk to you for a moment?"

"I guess."

I followed her to the kitchen.

"Listen, I know you and Troy used to be buds and all and I really want you to feel welcome here, but the energy you put out when you shushed me right then, like, in my own home, it was really violent. I felt violated. First you shushed me in my own home. And after that it's been attack after attack. My soul feels, well, it feels raped."

I apologized. I had never been accused of rape before. I felt awful.

She smiled. "I'm going to have to ask you to leave."

I walked back into the living room. Ta-Bone was doing made-up yoga moves on the floor. When I told him we had to leave he got upset, immediately breaking character.

"What the fuck, man," he said. "I was just getting my yoga boner all revved up."

Cassandra looked at him with eyes so intense I could have sworn I heard them hissing. He got up and ran up to me like a nervous child. He reminded me to ask Troy to buy us booze. I figured, at this point, I had nothing to lose.

So I told Troy about our situation and asked if he could help us out. The guy gave us a smile so kind I thought the booze was going to miraculously appear in the van. Instead he just asked us to leave.

As we were leaving he put his hands together and then bowed. "Namaste," he said.

EIGHT

I wanted a cherry Slurpee but all they had was Coke flavor, kiwi, and some other bullshit flavor. They never
have cherry when you truly need it. Whose idea was it
to make Coca-Cola and kiwi flavor? It seemed cruel. I
needed a pick-me-up. I needed a cherry flavored Slurpee.
The Yoga Masters had given my soul a wedgie. The joy-
ful part of my soul felt soggy.

We were all leaning against the minivan, trying to get
some fresh air.

"This Slurpee fucking sucks!" I yelled. I threw it and
watched it splatter on the pavement.

"What the fuck's your problem?" Ta-Bone asked.

"We should just call it quits," I said.

Ta-Bone stood really close to me. He was definitely in
my space bubble.

"I don't get you," he said. "Shit's been wild as hell. It's been a good night. And it will get better."

"It has not been a good night. It's been semi-traumatic for me."

"Cause you're a fucking pussy. Motherfuck, you got to smoke weed and eat pizza. You got attacked by rednecks. You got to see Ralph's magnificent shlong. That's all high adventure if you ask me. And all you have to do is find one person, just one person, to buy us booze and bring it to that party and you'll be popular, like me."

"Ta-Bone!" I yelled. "You're not popular!"

"Fuck you, Dr. Oldenstein. I'm popular. I'm like JFK. Everyone loves me."

"If you're so popular, then why are you hanging out with me? Why are you hanging out with Ralph?"

"I hang out with your old ass cause I like you, cause you didn't seem to give a shit. You're a fucking thirty-year-old man and you go to high school. I thought that was cool. I'm probably the only person that thought that was cool. But now I find out it wasn't just you trying to be crazy. I saw you with your friends. You're actually insecure. Ralph has more guts than you. People like me. I'm very likeable. I'm like Michael Jackson before he became all albino and started dressing like a nutcracker."

"You dress badly," I said. "You look like a twelve-year-old from the '90s."

That pushed him over the edge. He ran at me and tackled me onto the wet pavement. We wrestled around, not really taking a swing at each other. Finally, I pinned him.

Ralph jumped on as well. I don't think he knew we were fighting though. He kept yelling "Wrestlemania!" and "Pile driver!"

Ta-Bone tried to get out from under the pile.

"Get back here, demon child!" I yelled.

I grabbed his pants and undies and pulled back. He grabbed a lamppost and continued to pull himself out of the pile. I held onto his pants.

"Get the fuck off!" Ta-Bone yelled. "You pathetic old man!"

There was a brief tug of war. Next thing I knew I had his pants and underwear down around his ankles.

This old guy walked by and laughed. The owner of the 7-11 came out and told us to get away from his store.

I let go. He scrambled to his feet and pulled his pants and underwear back up.

A group of middle school girls were standing in front of the 7-11. They were laughing their asses off.

"BOOO!" they yelled. "TOO SMALL!"

I thought it looked fine. As a matter of fact, it looked a lot like my own dick. The two dicks could be twins. It was eerie.

"Hey," I said to the girls. "He's a grower not a shower."

"I don't even know what that means," one girl said.

I got up and walked up to my friend. A few other spectators had gathered. Ta-Bone gave them the finger.

"You okay?" I asked.

"Fuck off."

"Hey! Why did we stop wrestling?" Ralph yelled. "I

was having a good time."

We walked to the minivan.

"Let's get out of here," he said.

NINE

My friend, Craig, finally texted back. I had not talked to this guy in a long time. He had an apartment above the Japanese food place. He didn't live there full time, just on weekends when he wanted to get away from the city. I called the guy up and he sounded excited to hear from me. He invited me up.

Before we left, I noticed a truck at the other end of the parking lot. It was the mutants that tried to drive us off the road. One of them was standing outside the truck, staring off.

Craig was annoyed I brought teenagers with me. But he got over it quickly. They were so impressed with his fancy apartment. He loved being complimented.

"This place is awesome," Ralph said. "I want to lose

my virginity in a place like this. This place is so clean. It smells good."

"That's what all the ladies say," Craig said.

Ralph ran to the big flat screen TV. Craig turned it on for them and set up a video game for him to play. Ta-Bone joined in. He was still sulking. But once he started playing a video game he cheered up.

"Do you guys need me to do any laundry?" Craig asked.

That seemed like a random question.

"Why?" I asked.

"It looks like you guys have had a long day. Maybe you've developed an odor. I have a new machine that can wash and dry clothing in ten minutes. The thing's state of the art. I just wanted to show it to you. No big deal."

"We're fine," I said.

I saw him take a whiff. He tried to hide his disgust.

"I showered this morning."

"I'm sure."

"So how's the city?" I asked, trying to change the subject.

"Good. Great. Always great. The city is always great. It has this intensity. It's in the air. It tests you every day. And the women . . ."

"I know. I lived there once. Remember, we were roommates?"

"You did, sort of."

"Remember? I was there for a while."

"Only for a year. Doesn't really count. You have to

live in the city for at least three, four, maybe five years to see if you can really make it."

I laughed. "Five years? That's a really long time. Why would anyone live somewhere they hate for five years?"

He shrugged his shoulders and went to the refrigerator and pulled out a bottle of wine. He uncorked it and poured us both a glass.

"Can my friends get some wine?"

He looked at them and then back at me.

"No, that's weird."

"Why?"

"Too young. I feel weird just having them here. I feel like my apartment should have an age limit. Like a bar. You must be over 21 to enter."

"Twenty-one-year-olds are awful. Teenagers are fun."

"I can't tell the difference."

Ta-Bone saw me drinking wine and gave me a nasty look. I tried to ignore it.

"So, how's work?" I asked.

He sighed. "Hard. But rewarding. Mainly reviewing restaurants. I'm doing a book on hip restaurants in the Hamptons. It's a good time. They pay for me to go wherever I want."

"You still write fiction? Remember those hilarious poems you used to write?"

He looked like he had just eaten something that had gone bad. "Naw, a few years ago I came to a point where I was like, fuck it, it's okay to just focus on making money if that's what I want to do. And that's ok. That's part of maturing."

"Right. So where's Lila?"

"That bitch. She was a dud. Hopeless. I broke up with her and then dated this girl Kelly for a while. She was into rim jobs. But, you know how it is, anything can get boring. Even rim jobs. I still get to go to the club though. She's desperate to get me back. She doesn't have a chance though. Check this out."

He motioned for me to come close. He took out his iPhone and showed me a video. The screen showed a cock going in and out of a butthole. The ass barely made an appearance. The camera focused on the cock.

"The archive!" I said. "I forgot about the archive. You have any vids of Janet on this?"

"Sure."

"Dude, show me."

"No."

"What do you mean, no?"

"No."

"Why not? She's easily your most smoking hot ex. I've been dying to see a pic of this girl naked for years. Are you still hung up on her? Is that why you can't show me the pic?"

"No."

"Come on!"

"David, she's sixteen in the photos I have of her. Her vagina was pure. No ghost dick haunting her meaty caverns. Nowadays, she's as cheap as a haunted house at a carnival."

"That's mean," I said. "Shit, I saw her recently. She looked good. I'd still hook up with her."

"Did you just say 'hook up?' Dude, how old are you?"

"Fuck off."

He went back into his refrigerator and pulled out a plate of brownies and brought this to my friends in the living room. They scarfed them down and then went back to playing video games.

They were acting strange. It was as if he had turned them back into children.

"So have you thought about a career?" Craig asked.

"I'm a student," I said.

He smiled. "Right. High school. I heard about that. Amazing. Kids, did you know I have known David here since he was five?"

They paused the video game and looked up at Craig like he was Mr. Rogers. I hated the spell Craig put on people.

"Ever since he was young this kid has been the king of leisure. He managed to slack off when he was in kindergarten. Who manages to be a slacker when they're that young? When everyone else turned fourteen and went out to get jobs in restaurants and landscaping and cleaning pools, David went out and became a babysitter. When everyone else started going to college and taking it to the next level, he stayed home and ran a day care center. How many kids went to that? Like three? And you let them go there for free, because they were all poor as hell."

He talked like he was giving a toast, but everything he said felt bad. Having my life summed up like that was crushing. My soul felt like it had just sprained something and it was having trouble walking.

"And now he's in high school again. Well, no one could ever say you're not original. And you don't let things get to you. It's amazing. People say horrible things about this guy, but he's unfazed. He just keeps on chilling. King of leisure. Look at these tits."

He grabbed my man breasts. Ta-Bone was still mad and he wanted to laugh at me, I could tell. But he didn't.

"What! They don't teach Phys Ed in high school anymore?"

He laughed so loud it almost felt like the whole world was laughing as well.

Craig spent the next hour playing videogames with the kids. I tried to talk to him about my life. I tried to come across a little less like a slacker. He didn't seem interested.

The kids were impressed with his video gaming ability. They looked like they could watch him play that video game all night. But we had a mission. The party started in a couple hours. I had to break the spell.

"Listen, Craig, I need a favor."

"What, man? Anything. You know I got your back."

"We got this party to go to. I'm in charge of buying booze."

"That's great. You're learning how to be responsible."

"Right. Anyway, here's the problem. I lost my wallet. So don't have an ID. I was wondering if you could pick up the beer."

He got up and walked over to me. I pulled out the list.

He looked at it the way a dad looks over a crappy report card.

"What the fuck is this?" he said. "You call me for the first time in two years and you try to get me to buy alcohol for minors. Do you have any idea how inappropriate that is?"

"Listen man, if you don't—"

"You need to grow up!" he yelled. "This is bullshit."

"Chill out, man."

"Don't tell me to chill out in my own house. You come in here, stinking things up with your weird fat person smell. You drink my wine. And then you tell me to chill out?"

"I'm sorry, it's just . . ."

"Don't just be sorry. I want you to get your act together."

"I'm doing fine."

"Dude, you're still in high school. You're basically redefining what it means to be having a rough patch."

"I don't understand," Ralph said.

I looked over. Ralph was standing behind Craig.

"What don't you understand?"

Ralph scratched behind his ear and then smelled his finger. Craig cringed.

"He just wanted a favor," Ralph said. "You could just say no. Why are you yelling at him?"

"Sit down, you little mutant. You smell like pepperoni and foot fungus."

"Why do you have to be so mean?" he said.

"I'm not mean. I'm just honest. David needs to learn

that you can't just go through life having no ambition, no passion."

"That's bullshit," I said. "You *are* mean. You're one of the biggest pricks I know. And your honesty is shit. No one asked you to teach them any lessons. You're a dick. And I am more passionate about being a fuck up than you are about anything in your life!"

"I don't even know what that means."

I lunged at him. The two of us started wrestling. Usually Craig would have been able to whip my ass easily, but I had conjured up some secret anger strength and I was able to hold my own.

The kids jumped on top of us. I couldn't tell what was going on. Things got confusing. Ta-Bone's pants got pulled down again. His bare ass landed on my face. His balls plopped onto my forehead. I told him to move, but he couldn't. Craig had him in a headlock.

"I'm coming!" Ralph yelled.

We all stopped fighting and looked over at Ralph. His pants were around his ankles and his boner shot through his boxers.

"What are you doing?" I yelled.

"That thing is impressive," Craig said.

"I don't know what to do!" Ralph yelled. "My boner feels all weird. I'm scared."

"Dude, calm down," I said.

"What the fuck's wrong with this nerd?" Craig said.

There was a low rumbling. The sound seemed to come from the boy's ball sack.

"What the fuck is that?" Craig said.

"Stop yelling at me. I think I'm going to . . ."

A geyser of jizz burst out of the kid's massive wiener. No one was spared. Nerd spunk covered us. We all sat on the floor not talking, in shock.

"I think you all should leave," Craig said.

He walked to the bathroom and got in the shower. I could hear the water pouring over him. Craig hated getting dirty. He hated bodily fluids. He was going to be in there for a while.

Before we left we ran into Craig's room and stole a bunch of his clothes.

"What the fuck are you freaks doing?" I heard Craig yell from the shower. "Get the fuck out of my apartment!"

We took some clothes and ran to the minivan.

"What the fuck just happened back there?" Ta-Bone said.

"I don't know," Ralph said. "Everyone was fighting and I jumped on and I accidentally rubbed against someone's butt area. It felt too awesome. I thought something was wrong. So I pulled down my pants to see what was happening. Then I came."

Ralph sat in the front seat. He looked dazed. He had not gotten any jizz on himself, but he changed anyway. The clothing was too big for him, but he looked snazzy.

"Am I a freak?" he asked. "What if the only way I can cum is to get into a fight?"

I told him he was fine, and we drove off.

TEN

We passed the Headlights Bar and Grill. A group of people stood outside smoking. There was a line outside of Sen, the Japanese food place. I had never actually been in there. Most of my friends had worked there at one point or another, but I had never been able to afford it.

I drove out of town and down Route 117, then down to Payne Avenue, and up Cliffords Street. There were no cops on this street and I wanted to drive fast.

I saw a pair of headlights pull up behind us. It pulled up close. It was a truck. I could see the front bumper. It looked like teeth.

It was the mutants.

"Oh no," Ralph said. "It's them again."

They honked their horn and then pulled up next to me. The mutant in the front passenger seat had his naked ass hanging out the window. It was an unsettling pale thing. The anus was a puke-ish shade of green. The mutant's asshole pulsated. It opened and closed, making it look like a baby bird begging for food.

"Fuck off!" I yelled.

A small nugget of shit fell out of the pulsating butthole. We all screamed. The gnarly hole continued to huff and puff and then a much thicker turd came out.

They sped up.

"Finally they're gone," Ralph said. "I just want to go home."

"This isn't over," I said.

"What do you mean?"

I stepped on the gas.

"Condescending motherfuckers!" I yelled.

"Buttcrack, no!" Ralph's voice sounded shaky and nervous. "I think you have some misplaced anger. Maybe we should just pull over and talk or . . ."

"Never!" I yelled.

I drove the minivan alongside the truck. The mutants looked over at me. They were confused. Maybe even a little scared.

"Pull over!" I yelled.

Before they could respond, the road curved sharply and I lost control of the vehicle.

When I finally woke up I was sprawled out on a wooden floor. I felt weak. My head ached. I tested each part of my body to make sure I was okay. I was stiff, but I could move each finger, toe, each limb. I could move my neck.

THE PARTY LORDS

My face felt lumpy. There was dry blood covering my hands and my face. But other than that, I could move everything I needed to move.

I looked around, hoping to find my friends alive and with me. I looked around the room. Blankets covered the walls. One of the mutants was sitting on a broken down La-Z-Boy.

The guy had a head like an albino Klingon. His arms hung to his sides. They were apish, twice the length of a normal man's arms. And they looked strong. I had never seen so many muscles.

I shut my eyes again and lay there, still pretending to be unconscious. I tried to think of some way to get away without the mutants seeing me. I took another peek. There were no windows. Just walls covered in blankets. There was a flashlight hanging from the ceiling. There was a door. But I had no idea where it led.

The guy snorted like a pig. I closed my eyes again. Part of me wanted to just get up and run. But I kept still. I waited. I needed some sort of plan.

I heard footsteps. Most likely it was another mutant. Maybe this one was going to start cutting me up and cooking me. I took another peek. A naked woman stood over freaky-ape-arms. Her face was pointy, like a rat. She carried a steak knife in one hand and a pair of pliers in the other.

The woman growled at the man and he growled back. I shut my eyes again. I tried to keep them shut. But I couldn't. I needed to know what was going on.

Ratface brought the plier up to a pimple on the guy's chin. She squeezed it. Blood and pus shot out and hit her in the face. She moaned.

She found another zit on his head. She popped it.

And another.

There was a potato-sized boil on his chest. She lowered the knife and carved the boil open. Pus puffed out of the boil like whip cream. I had never seen so much pus. It made the whole room smell like feet and tuna fish. The woman took the pus in her hand. The man smiled. His dick got hard. She grabbed his boner and jerked the guy off using the pus as lube.

I gagged and closed my eyes hoping for the scene to pass. The man moaned. He sounded like a puppy begging for food.

I opened my eyes again. I don't know why. The man was just sitting there, dick soft and dripping. He looked worn out. The woman wasn't done. She squeezed more pus out of the boil. There was so much of the goopy stuff. There seemed to be an endless supply. She ate some, like it was Fluff, and then rubbed the rest of the nasty ass goopiness on her body. It made her look shiny and awful.

I gagged. This time she heard me. She looked over and saw that I was awake. She squealed. I got up and backed into the corner of the room. She rushed up to me and started sniffing my body.

I apologized. I didn't know what I was apologizing for, but I kept saying "I'm sorry!" over and over again.

"Just let me go," I begged.

THE PARTY LORDS

The guy in the chair laughed.

The woman continued sniffing me. She especially liked the way my dick area smelled. Her nose sounded like a vacuum cleaner. She took it all in.

After sniffing away on my dingus, she took my hand and put a scoop of mutant pus in it. The stuff was warm and oily. I shuddered and begged God for help. The woman took my hand and rubbed it into her mutant cooter. I tried to pull my fingers out, but her vagina squeezed onto it. I had never felt such strong pussy muscles. It felt like the handshake Annie's husband, Mike, gave me. I yelled out what I wanted to yell when Mike shook my hand. "Help!" I screamed. "Help!"

Ratface started screaming as well. So did Ape Arms. Only they screamed like porno chicks. They weren't scared. They were coming. My screaming made them cum.

The door opened.

Another mutant entered. He was a big three-hundred pounder. His face was wrinkly, like an old woman, but the rest of him was firm muscle. A boy stood beside him. He stepped into the light. It was Ta-Bone.

"Buttcrack!" he said. "You gotta meet the rest of these freaks. These guys are rad. Seriously, we've been getting rowdy as hell. Come on out. They're chill."

ELEVEN

We gathered in the kitchen. I was really on edge. I was still kinda upset from being molested and all that. Ta-Bone assured me everything was okay. He had a bump on his head and a few scrapes, but otherwise he was fine. They hadn't tortured him at all. Ralph looked completely unharmed. There were a few bruises, a few scrapes, but other than that, he looked happy. The kid was always happy. He had that vacant I-don't-know-what-the-fuck-is-going-on kinda happiness. But this was different. This was better. It was a better sort of happiness. He kept telling the mutants about all the gross things he did and they thought it was hilarious.

There was one woman they called Momma Poonshine. She sat at the end of a long table. She was super fat. She might have been the fattest woman I had ever seen. Other than that, she was the most normal-looking of the people in the kitchen.

She gave me some pills.

"What the fuck are these?" I asked.

"Go on honey, it's just ibuprofen."

One of the freaks came up. He pulled up his shirt and showed me his massive nipples.

"What the fuck's your problem?" I said.

"Don't be an ass," Ta-Bone said. "For real, everyone is chill here."

The man started crying.

"He don't know how to talk much," Momma said. "Most of us can't talk."

"Why?"

"Too much drink. It's changed us."

"Booze fucked up your vocal cords?"

She laughed. It was a beautiful, hardy laugh. Except she drooled a lot. That was kinda gross.

"No, not booze—drink. We made this drink. Let me tell you about the drink."

She explained their situation. The McMurtrys had been living in this area for years. They weren't inbred. Well, they were a little inbred, but that wasn't why they were all fucked up-looking. That was not where the mutations began. They had made this drink they called Big Fun. It was kinda like moonshine, only it tasted better and it didn't fuck you up in the same way. They claimed it was the smoothest, most rowdiest party drink ever. But it had some fucked up side effects. They drank too much

Big Fun. After a year or so they started to change. They started to mutate in ways that made them look all inbred and shit. And the women started giving birth to nine and ten babies at a time and they all grew up super fast. By the time they were five they looked full-grown. And funny looking. The Big Fun made them funny looking. It also fucked up their vocal cords, making it so they couldn't talk.

Years passed. They continued drinking the Big Fun. "We love to party!" Momma said.

They didn't leave the compound much though. They were afraid of how people would treat them. They felt ashamed.

"But I think I saw some of you at school today," I said. "And what about the guys in the truck?"

"Those are our little ones. The little ones don't get as ashamed."

"How little are they?"

"They're only six years old or so."

I pointed to the big muscle man with the grandma face. "And him?"

"He's a little older. Eleven."

I noticed Ta-Bone had a glass of it. He was sitting on a woman's knee getting a back massage from her weird flipper hands.

"You shouldn't drink that," I said.

They assured me the Big Fun would not affect you the first bunch of times you drank it. In fact, you had to drink it consistently for years for it to start changing your body in any way.

"Why do you keep drinking the stuff?" I asked.

"Cause we like to party is all," she said. "Can't blame us for liken us some fun times."

I looked over at Ralph. He looked so at home. He showed a few of the mutants a big ball of earwax he had pulled out of his ear. They loved it. They clapped and cheered and howled. The whole scene would have seemed downright wholesome if they hadn't just molested me with zit pus.

"They got so much of that weird drink," Ta-Bone said. "Check it out!"

They took me to a back room. Hundreds of bottles of the stuff sat on the shelves. The stuff practically shined.

"They weren't trying to fuck with us before," Ta-Bone said. "They were just playing around."

I walked to the door and looked outside. There were dozens of shanty houses spread out over a large field. Mutants were everywhere. They stumbled around holding jugs of Big Fun. Their faces and limbs were all out of whack. They looked like reflections in a fun house mirror.

"You got to see the rest of this place," Ta-Bone said. "They got a full town here. Its rowdy as hell. The whole town is nuts. It's like fucking spring break up in this motherfucker."

"What about Ralph?"

"He'll be fine," he said.

Ta-Bone, Grandma-face and I walked around the shantytown, while she continued to explain things to me.

"For real, these guys are all sustainable too. How awesome is that? Look, they got their own farm and shit."

They walked me to the barn. All the animals were mutated. Did they feed the animals Big Fun too? Ta-Bone told me they did. Big Fun was apparently rich in vitamins.

Outside the barn, I saw two of the mutants rough housing. They were wearing nothing but oversized shirts. They gave each other wedgies and noogies and all the traditional stuff. Then one bit off the other's ear. The injured mutant howled in pain. Blood spat out of the side of his head. His blood was thicker than usual. Most likely a result of drinking Big Fun.

They continued rough housing. The earless one bit off the other's right nipple. Grandma-face laughed and cheered them on. The two boys stopped wrestling. They looked, examined each other's wounds, laughed, and then hugged.

The mutants played rough. Maybe they didn't mean to terrorize people. Maybe they were just joking around when they pissed on the minivan, or showed us their asshole or drove us off the road.

It was only ten at night. It felt much later. We gathered in the kitchen again. Ta-Bone sat on flipper lady's lap. She put her flipper hand down his pants and fiddled around with his boner. He looked content.

Ralph showed momma a smell he had found behind his ear. "It's not a sexy thing, but it still smells bad, check it out."

He put his finger under her nose.

She smelled it and smiled.

"Mmmm, it does smell bad," she said. "I think it's very sexy."

Grandma-face brought us all big mugs of the stuff.

I took a sip. It tasted good. It tasted really good. It tasted like pussy juice. Fatty explained that pussy was one of the main ingredients.

I continued drinking. The buzz it gave me was awesome. I felt goofy and warm and a little speedy.

Ralph laughed.

"What's so funny?"

He pointed at my crotch. I had my dick out. Damn, this stuff relaxed you too much.

We all laughed. All of us. The mutants. Ralphy. Ta-Bone. All of us.

TWELVE

I figured I had ruined Perfect Kid's party. I imagined that I was the only way they were ever going to get alcohol. When we got there though, the party was in full swing. Everyone was drunk. They had managed to snag booze from his parents' secret stash. It was enough to get most of them buzzed. But they were running low. So they were grateful to see me.

They weren't so excited to see who I had with me. I had Grandma-face, Flipper Lady, Ape Arms, and a few others. They were the chillest of the group. The others were already too drunk to leave the compound. Momma mutant stayed home to look after them. That seemed to be her role.

"What the fuck, man," Perfect Kid said. "What's with your crew?"

"They're my buddies," I said.

THE PARTY LORDS

"What are these, Ralph's cousins or something? They look fucked up."

"No, just some kids we met tonight. They like to party!"

One of the mutants tried to speak, but all he could say was "PARRRRRRRREEEEEEE!"

"They like to party, but they don't speak so well."

"I don't know about this, man. And you brought Ta-Bone. That kid's annoying. And why are you all fucked up-looking? There's blood on your shirt."

"It's a long story."

"Listen man, this is all a bit much, bro. I mean, your crew is annoying and scary and . . ."

"I thought you were all open minded," I said.

"I am, but dude, these guys look like murderers."

"Listen, we got a ton of weird mutant booze we would love to share. But if you want us to leave . . ."

I showed him a bottle. Grownups hate sketchy drugs, but teenagers love them. They love feeling as sneaky as possible. Naturally, the Big Fun was intriguing to him.

"Let me try it," he said.

He took a sip. His eyes lit up. "This is amazing." He took another sip. "It's downright spiritual and shit."

Once Perfect Kid said he liked it, I knew we were in.

"Ok, you can tell your friends they can stay. But no gross *Wrong Turn* shit."

We walked inside and everyone stopped what they were doing and looked at us suspiciously. They were all dressed so nicely and looked so hip. We looked like we were radioactive things from the apocalypse. I'm sure we looked sinister to them. They needed Perfect Kid to tell them everything was okay, that we weren't going to kidnap them and torture them and eat them. They needed him to assure them we were creepy in a cool way, not a depressing or scary way. If he seemed annoyed, we would be ignored all night long. If he looked angry we might get into a fight. Luckily, Perfect Kid treated us like we were royalty from a foreign land. He was in love with the Big Fun.

"Look what they brought!" He held up a jug of the stuff.

He passed it around and some of his friends took sips. Their eyes widened.

"This shit's awesome," one kid said.

A girl took a swig. "It tastes familiar. I can't quite place it. But it's delicious."

Perfect Kid looked back at me. "What's this called again?"

"Big Fun."

He held up the jug.

"Big Fun!" he yelled.

Everyone cheered. They didn't even know what the stuff was. It didn't matter. They could tell by the look on his face that it was fun, and that the party was about to get crazier. They liked that.

The mutants were surprisingly nervous. They hid behind us like they were little kids, which, I guess they were. Drooly had a full beard, but he was only four.

Ralph and Ta-Bone introduced them to people as they

handed out the Big Fun.

And everyone loved the Big Fun. The effect was like alcohol, but it made people seem sexier and feel sexier. And it had that speedy quality. The first sip was like snorting a line of cocaine. It left you all freaked out and wide-eyed and excited. Plus it tasted great.

The mutants noticed some kids dancing in the living room. It got them excited. They started moving around, trying to imitate them. Once the mutants started dancing everyone else joined in.

I started dancing too. At this point I was on my second bottle of Big Fun and I felt like I was possessed by some ancient party God. A girl came up to me and danced close. I grabbed her butt. It was little. "You're old!" she said. I smiled like it was a compliment.

I danced my way into the center of the party. I kept grabbing ass. There was so much of it. At one point I grabbed Perfect Kid's ass. I didn't care. It felt good. I grabbed it again. He thought it was funny.

I saw someone swinging from a chandelier and, for a moment, I was worried one of the mutants had gotten a little too wild. It wasn't one of the mutants, though. It was a high school kid.

One of the mutants did get a little too wild. He started humping the couch. Everyone thought it was funny though. This chubby chick started spanking the mutant's ass.

A hippie girl came up to me. I loved her smell. I usually like chicks that bathe, but that night I felt more animal-

istic. I liked her weird animal smells. I think it was the
Big Fun's fault. I think it was the Big Fun that was
making me like this stinky girl.

"Thanks so much for all the awesome homebrewed
beer. I love homebrewed shit," this hippie girl said. "It's
the dankness."

She started dancing and rubbing her butt on me. The
music was loud. They played nothing but rap. Rap had
gotten a lot sleazier and goofier since I was a kid. I liked
that.

The hippie girl kept dancing. She put her crotch on
my leg and moved back and forth like I was a rocking
horse.

One of the mutants crept up behind her and started
chewing on one of her dreads. When she saw him, she
smiled and then reached back and grinded her ass against
him.

More kids showed up. The place was packed. I needed
fresh air. I was sweaty and needed more Big Fun anyway.

I walked outside and found our truck. I grabbed some
Big Fun and headed out back. Perfect Kid had a massive
pool. Ralph stood on the diving board. He was wearing
nothing but his boxers.

"Cannonball!" he yelled.

He jumped in, made a splash, and climbed out and up
onto the diving board again. Another student snuck up
behind him. He pulled down his pants. Ralph looked
embarrassed until everyone started cheering.

"Holy shit, look at the size of that thing!" one girl yelled.

"Moby dick!" they started chanting. "Moby dick! Moby dick!"

He took his shorts off and threw them aside. The dong hung low. It looked even bigger and more dong-like than usual. I felt an intense sense of pride.

"Moby dick!" I yelled.

The crowd continued chanting.

"MOBY DICK! MOBY DICK!"

One of the mutants came up to me. He looked at Ralph's dangling meat-broom. The mutant had a tiny face and couldn't talk. But he tried. He started chanting.

"Moooooget! Mooooooogetty!"

Ralph looked over at me, smiled, and jumped in the pool again.

Ta-Bone came up to me. He looked completely hammered.

"You old so and so. Look at you. Look at your curvy ass. You're so touchable. You been dancing the night away, haven't you motherfucker?"

"I've been dancing a little."

He put his arm around me. "I made love to one of those mutant chicks," he said. "Does that make me an inbred?"

I laughed. "No," I said. "I don't think that's how it works."

I saw a mutant girl in the background. Her dress was falling off. Her nipples were poking out. They were extra long nipples too. Those things looked like little red antennae. Those things looked like they shot milk out like a Super Soaker 20.

"Look at her. I sucked those titties so hard. She loved it. She loved my sweaty little ding dong too."

She growled at us. I couldn't tell if she was angry or not. Her beady eyes made her emotions hard to read. Ta-Bone smiled at her though. He liked her.

"I'll be there in a moment, baby. I'm just having some man time. Chill for a second. Damn."

A girl walked by, took off her clothes, and jumped in the pool naked. Ta-Bone and I looked at the girl, then each other. We laughed, high fived, hugged, and did everything we could to tell each other that we were having the best time ever.

Ta-Bone put his hand on my shoulder. "Listen man, I just want to tell you that even though you can be annoying as fuck sometimes, that you are my best friend and I promise you that when I get older I will not be like Craig or any of those guys."

I smiled. "It's okay," I said. "Those guys aren't so bad."

"Come over here," he said.

We hugged. It felt nice, cozy, devoid of homesickness. I tried to let go, but he wouldn't let me. We hugged until we both felt too uncomfortable. By the time he let go, we were both crying a little.

"Damn, that moment was emotional as hell. That was some *Fried Green Tomatoes* shit."

"You've seen *Fried Green Tomatoes*?" I asked.

THE PARTY LORDS

"Fucking FGT is the shit," he said. "That thing is like my favorite movie ever."

I decided to go in for a second hug. Ta-Bone gave good hugs. It felt manly in all the right ways.

THIRTEEN

More people came. The party spilled out onto the street. The mutants went back for more Big Fun. People were getting nuts. They brought speakers outside. Everyone danced and jumped around and acted wild as hell. But, like Perfect Kid had said, there were no neighbors, so we could be as loud and ape-shit crazy as we wanted.

I ran into an older guy near the pool. "Look at that girl's rear end," he said. "It fills me with the love of the gods."

Holy shit, it was Troy.

"WUZZZZ UP?" I said.

He put his arm around me. "Did you bring this fine drink?" he asked.

He had a jug of Big Fun in his hand.

"I did, I did."

"It is a fine drink," he said.

We embraced.

"Where is Cassandra?"

"I'm so tired of her," he said. "All she does is meditate and do yoga and cook awful food. Sometimes you have to go out and party!"

We raised our jugs. "Hell yeah!" I said.

A girl walked by. She was tall and goofy-looking, but also kinda sexy.

"I must follow that girl and sunbathe in her inner light," he said.

"Go for it!" I said.

He winked at me.

"You have a good soul," he said.

"No shit, you think so?"

He winked again. This wink seemed kinda perverted.

I walked to the mutants' truck to get some more Big Fun. I had finished three bottles of it and I felt beyond wasted, but I didn't feel sick and didn't feel too sloppy. I was still in that overconfident stage of drunkenness. But was I even drunk? Does Big Fun get you drunk, or was this something else? I couldn't tell. At times it felt like an entirely different sensation, other times I just felt like I was partying.

Two kids were sitting on the back of the truck. They were Annie's kids. They each had a jug of Big Fun.

"What the fuck are you doing here?"

"Chilling," said one of the little demons.

"You two are way too young for this party," I said.

"Eat my beaver, old man," the other one said.

I don't think they knew what a beaver was.

"How did you get here anyway?"

"We rode our bikes. Now get your bitch tits out of here."

"I need to get some more Big Fun."

"That will be five dollars."

One of the kids held out his hand to collect the cash.

"Are you shitting me?"

He smiled.

I handed him five bucks and he handed me a jug of Big Fun.

A girl walked by and the boys started heckling her.

"Hey baby, you want some Doublemint gum?"

The girl rolled her eyes.

"As if," the girl said.

The brothers high-fived.

There were lots of naked girls near the pool, so I chilled over there. At one point, I looked at my phone and saw that there were dozens of phone calls from Vicki. I tried to call her back but a kid bumped into me, knocking my cell phone into the pool. Everyone looked at me like something truly horrible had just happened.

"Fuck it!" I yelled.

Everyone cheered.

I told the mutants not to molest anyone or fight or pop any zits. But things got so crazy and I got so drunk on Big Fun I just didn't care what happened.

After dropping my cell phone in the pool I was feeling

fully awesome in every way. I walked inside to dance and
grab more ass. To get to the living room, I had to pass
through the kitchen.

I found Ape Arms sitting on the kitchen table. He had
cut open one of his boils and was draining it. The kids
loved it. They were gagging, but in an enthusiastic way.
They didn't use it as lube, thank God. They just thought
it was funny. The more he squeezed, the more pus poured
out and the more they laughed and gagged and cheered.

I had to piss. I mean I had to piss more than I had ever
had to piss in my life. I ran upstairs. There was a line. I
pushed my way past. The door was locked. I kicked it
open. This kid was doing his girlfriend. He had her bent
over the sink.

I closed the door and then apologized to the young
lovers and started to piss.

The dude waited. He kept his dick in the girl.

"Do you mind?" she said.

I gave her a wink before the piss started flooding out
of me and kept pouring out.

"Holy shit, man. Are you okay?" the boy asked.

I smiled. "Best piss of my life," I said.

It continued to pour out.

"Wow, this is kinda hot," the girl said.

I walked out of the bathroom and pushed my way
through all the teens. I was so drunk, but I wasn't stum-
bling. That's the magic of Big Fun, I guess. A group of
teens gathered around this one door. I walked up to see

what they were listening to.

"Take it," I heard a drunk lady say.

That voice sounded familiar. I opened the door slightly and looked inside.

It was Vicki. She had a turkey baster up this mutant's butt.

The teenagers laughed. Vicki looked over and saw me.

"David! It's not what you think!"

The mutant made a grunting noise. He didn't want her to stop reaming him out.

Vicki ran up to me. She was really drunk.

"What are you doing here?" I asked.

"Baby, I'm sorry. I got so mad at you earlier. I came here to apologize. Then this crazy booze got passed around. I might have gotten a wee bit too drunk and then I started dancing with this dude. And one thing led to another."

I smiled.

The kids were still standing there, listening intently.

"Are you mad?" she asked.

"I don't know," I said. "Does this mean that I'm off the hook?"

"What do you mean?"

"Can I hook up with someone else tonight?"

"I guess."

The mutant cried out to her. His butthole needed attention.

"Go finish off on your new guy. I'm not mad. I'm sure I'll be all sad and confused tomorrow. But let's just have a good time tonight."

THE PARTY LORDS

"You sure, baby?"

"I'm sure."

The teens cheered. Teenagers love cheering.

I closed the door and the moaning noises continued.

"Take it!" I heard her yell. "Take it and love it!"

FOURTEEN

I found Perfect Kid and asked him about the girl who had the locker next to mine. I felt beyond confident. I just needed to find the girl and then I would make something happen. All insecurity had drowned in the Big Fun.

"She has a big butt," I told him. "It's maybe the best booty in the entire world."

"I think all booties are the best booties in the world. All booties are equal when it comes to the soul."

"No, this one's even better though."

"I don't know man. You got to be more specific."

"I call her Rhino Booty."

"That's kinda messed up."

"She's pretty," I said. "She has a face like an owl."

"Oh, you mean Renee?"

"Is that her name?"

"How do you not know her name, dude?"

"I don't know. Is she here?"

He led me to the garage. There were two tables set up for beer pong. Rhino Booty was at one of the tables. Her butt looked big and wonderful.

She looked up and recognized me and ran up and hugged me like we were old friends.

"You came," she said.

"He was the one that brought this awesome home brewed beer."

"Well it's not really . . ."

She hugged me again. "I'm so glad you're here."

I was surprised she knew who I was. We had been running into each other for months, but we had rarely talked. It seemed like she just thought I was a cutie. A thirty-year-old cutie that was still in high school. This was one open minded girl. It must have been the Big Fun. That stuff is magic. That stuff makes dreams come true.

We wandered the party and drank and talked. All of a sudden I felt like I was on a date. Only it wasn't awkward. Everything we said seemed like pure comedy. It was one of the finest giggle sessions I had ever had.

We went to the pool and put our feet in. We talked as the party raged around us.

"So what's it like being all grown up?" She asked.

"I don't know," I said. "It sounds awful though."

She laughed.

"So you don't think of yourself as a grownup?" she

asked.

"No."

"Old guys like my butt, it's a proven fact. But since you don't think you're actually grown up, I guess you don't like me."

"Oh, no, I love your butt. It's one of the best butts I have ever seen."

She gave me a sneaky look. She knew I liked her. She knew I wanted to make sweet, tender dorky old man love and, if she would let me, maybe even cry a little bit afterward. She knew this. I could tell by the way she looked at me.

"Why do you hang out with that Ta-Bone kid so much?" she asked.

"He reminds me of the kids I grew up with."

"I heard that Ralph kid has a big cock."

"I can ask him to show it to you."

"Really?"

"Sure."

"Do you have a big cock?"

"No, mine's pretty standard. It's your regular ol government-issued six-incher."

She laughed.

A naked girl walked by and jumped in the pool. I tried my hardest not to look at her too much and to focus on Renee. I wanted to keep things feeling romantic.

"What's the most awkward sex you ever had?" Renee asked.

"I don't know."

"Come on, you never had awkward sex?"

"Of course I have. Most of my sex is awkward. I kinda like it that way."

"Bullshit."

"Or at least I want to like it that way. Sometimes I get really annoyed about everything. Sometimes I hate how awkward sex can be. But then there are times when I love it. There are times when awkward sex is the best thing in the world. I try to feel that way all the time, but it's not easy."

"I don't know what the fuck you're talking about. I kinda wish you just answered my question."

"Ok, let me see. Ta-Bone caught me getting a turkey baster shoved up my ass."

"What? When?"

"Earlier today."

"Shut the fuck up!"

She laughed so hard she snorted.

"It wasn't my proudest moment."

"It should be," she said. "That's the funniest shit I've ever heard. I have never taken anything that big in my butt. Once I put some Tylenol in there."

"Why?"

"I wanted to see what it would be like to be a drug mule. I wanted to see if I had what it takes."

"That's fucked."

She pushed me. I fell backwards onto the grass.

"You're calling me fucked? You're the one taking the turkey baster in the butt."

We looked at each other and tried to hold back our laughter. It wasn't easy. Her face got all red and goofy-looking. Her eyes watered. She leaned down and kissed me.

Random kids kept coming up and bothering us. We needed some privacy. Perfect Kid's father had a shed. It was locked. We had a good time breaking the lock with rocks we found lining the garden.

As soon as we were inside she kissed me. It was a sloppy kiss, but I liked it.

I bent her over the lawn mower and tugged her tight jeans down. Her ass looked even better naked. I kneeled down and gave it a loving sniff. It was the perfect combo of ass sweat and poon juice.

"What are you doing?" she said. "Don't smell it."

"I like the smell."

She laughed, then snorted, then started breathing heavily.

I leaned over and put my face in between those two glorious ass cheeks. I licked around. There was a dingleberry. Even on the Big Fun, it was hard to find a dingleberry to be sexy. I refused to let it ruin the experience. I had to act fast. I bit the thing off and she yelped.

"What are you doing down there?" she asked.

I spit the dingleberry into the corner of the shed.

"Nothing," I said.

I went back down. I put my face even deeper into her ass. I found the pussy. I licked around. It wasn't a very productive pussy eating session. She did not come. There was no technique. I was like a dog drinking water. The sweetness made me feel giggly like a child.

FIFTEEN

Renee!" I heard someone yell in the distance.

I pulled my face out of her ass. I felt dizzy. Renee looked confused for a moment, then she heard her name being called again and she knew exactly who it was.

"Is that my Uncle Phil?"

"Renee!" the voice called out again.

"Your uncle is the gym teacher?"

She nodded.

We stepped out of the tool shed. Mr. Phillips stood in front of us. All the teenagers had gathered around. It was like the whole high school was there. Mr. Phillips grabbed me by the hair and dragged me through the crowd.

"You vile, pathetic excuse for a man," he said.

He threw me to the ground. The crowd came in closer. I didn't know what to say. The man felt violated. I had dry humped his sister. Now I was eating his niece's ass out. Both acts seemed sweet to me. To him I was a molester.

"Get up dude, kick that motherfucker's ass!" I heard one kid yell.

The crowd cheered. I felt like I was in *Rocky*, but that I hadn't changed and this was the alternate ending where he gets beaten to death.

I got up. He hit me in the gut. I keeled over. He slugged me in the head a couple of times. I fell, then staggered back, amazed this killing machine wasn't able to knock me out with a single hit.

"I'm going to have you thrown in prison!" he yelled.

"Uncle Phil," Renee said. "What are you doing?"

"How could you do this, Renee? Don't you have any self-respect?"

"Fuck you!" she yelled.

She burst into tears. She ran at him. He backhanded her. She fell on the ground and wept.

I ran at him, screaming. I hit him in the stomach a bunch of times. He grabbed me, pulled me in, lifted me up and threw me on the ground.

I lay there. He kicked me in the gut.

"Stop!" Renee yelled.

He straddled me and began to pound on my face. I was drunk on the Big Fun, but it still hurt.

"Get away from my friend!" I heard Ralph's nervous voice call out.

I looked up. He was standing there. He was naked and his dong was hard as hell.

"MOBY DICK!" the crowd chanted.

"What the hell are you doing?" Mr. Phillips said.

"Get up and leave!" Ralph said. Tears formed in his eyes. "We were having a good time. Buttcrack is a good guy. You should leave."

"It's okay, Ralph," I said. "Put your dick away, everything's . . ."

Mr. Phillips slugged me.

"Oh God, it's happening again!"

Mr. Phillips slugged me again and again.

"PLEASE, JUST LEAVE HIM ALONE!" Ralph yelled.

Jizz shot out of his dick. I had never in my life shot a load like that. It was like a bazooka. The jizz hit Mr. Phillips in the eye. The man fell back, landed on the ground and lay there holding his eye.

The crowd loved it. Their chanting got louder. "MOBY DICK! MOBY DICK! MOBY DICK!"

Mr. Phillips put his hand over his eye.

"It burns!" he yelled.

Ta-Bone came out of the crowd and ran at the bukkaked gym teacher. He kicked him a couple of times, but Mr. Phillips grabbed his leg and pulled him down and head butted him. Blood sprayed out of the boy's nose like a shaken up beer can. Ta-Bone cried hysterically.

His mutant girlfriend saw this and came to his rescue. She jumped on Mr. Phillips and bit his ear. He grabbed her and threw her off. She landed on all fours, his ear in her mouth. She chewed on it. The crowd groaned for a moment, but then began to cheer. But now their cheering didn't seem youthful or fun-spirited at all. They seemed crazed. Blood-thirsty.

Mr. Phillips covered his wound with his hand and staggered around. When he pulled himself together, he came at me again. This time old Grandma-face got him. The giant mutant pounded Mr. Phillips until his body was limp.

"You freak," Mr. Phillips mumbled through his mashed up lips.

Grandma-face put his mouth around Mr. Phillips' eyes. He sucked his eyeball right out of his socket. The gym teacher howled. The man was so hurt up. Grandma-face spit the eyeball into the air. The large mutant took Mr. Phillips and hammered on him.

Renee ran up to him and begged him to stop.

"He's killing him!"

I stumbled up to Grandma-face. I told him to stop, but he didn't listen.

Grandma-face picked up our gym teacher's unconscious body and held it above him like a trophy. The crowd watched in awe, then they broke into wild applause.

SIXTEEN

The teenagers were crazed on Big Fun. They started breaking everything. The pool was filled with furniture. Panties dangled from the trees like Christmas ornaments.

Renee was crying. She had her uncle in her arms. He was a mess.

"Help me," he said.

I don't think he knew who I was. I called over to Ta-Bone. He and I dragged Mr. Phillips through the woods and away from the party. Once we were a safe distance away, we got out of the woods and back on the road and Ta-Bone called a cab.

"I'm sorry," I said.

"It's not your fault."

We could hear the party in the distance.

"You know I can't date you, right?"

"I know."

I saw a pair of headlights. It was the cab.

We stood up. The car pulled up and the cabby rolled down his window. It was Lewis. Ta-Bone had fucking called Lewis's cab company.

"What the fuck is this?" he said when he saw Mr. Phillips.

"Just get him to the hospital and then get her home," I said.

"What the hell is going on?" he asked.

"Just do it. You owe me. I've driven your drunk ass home plenty of times when we used to hang."

He rolled his eyes.

We put Mr. Phillips in the cab. Renee got in the front seat.

"You want me to come with?" I asked.

"I think it's best if you don't," she said.

"I understand."

I watched them speed away and then headed back to the party.

They had made a massive bonfire out of all sorts of crap. It was huge. The flames went up thirty feet. Troy was dancing around the flames and chanting some crazy shit. Perfect Kid was with him. He was banging on a bucket like it was a drum.

I saw one of Annie's twins up in a tree. The other one was riding on the shoulders of some random tall chick.

Everyone looked like they had gone completely ape-shit nuts.

THE PARTY LORDS

"This is fucking awesome," Ta-Bone said.

We found Ralph and then looked around for the mutants, but they were all gone. They had snuck off in the middle of the chaos.

Ta-Bone wanted to go search the woods.

"We'll never find her," I said.

"We should at least try."

I heard sirens. It was the police.

"Maybe we should head into the woods," I said.

Ralph followed us. We wandered around, talking about love and fighting and Ralph's massive cock and how awesome it was. We talked about the party and how deranged everyone got at the end. We decided it was the Big Fun. It had to be the Big Fun.

It was dark. I had never seen anything so dark. We had our cell phones, but they didn't offer much light.

I kept asking my friends questions. As long as I kept them talking I didn't feel so scared. As long as I kept us all talking, I didn't care that I was completely lost.

SEVENTEEN

Morning came. Once it was light out, I could tell where I was. I had played in these woods since I was a kid. I used to hide here and smoke cigarettes and play Truth or Dare. I sucked my first boobs in these woods. They belonged to a girl named Maggie. She had her bra on, so really, I just sucked on her bra, but as far as my friends were concerned, it counted.

I led us to a place I called Fairytown. Craig and I made it when we were pre-teens. We made an entire city out of rocks and twigs. Some of the houses got elaborate. Craig was really into it. He built little fairy mansions. Then we'd show his little sister. She loved it. She would stomp around pretending she was a giant monster. She would knock down the fairy houses and Craig would get mad and yell at her. Then we'd rebuild them.

Some of the houses were still there. Some of them

looked new. Maybe some other kids had shown up and added to it.

"This place is creepy," Ta-Bone said.

"It's Fairytown."

"It looks more like a fucking fairy graveyard."

I studied the houses more. This was definitely Craig's handiwork. I laughed. I loved the idea of that yuppie sneaking into the woods and making fairy houses.

After Fairytown I brought us to my old house. There was a truck in the parking lot. I wondered who lived there. Part of me wanted to wait until that person woke up. I just wanted to see them.

But the kids were hungry. We walked to town. I wanted to buy them some breakfast but I had no money.

We stood in the parking lot of the Princess Diner staring off like we were amazed it was morning and the party had ended.

I saw a Saab with the top down peel into the parking lot.

"Is that your girlfriend?" Ralph asked.

Vicki was standing on the passenger seat. Craig was driving.

He pulled up to us and lowered his sunglasses.

"I heard you guys had a wild night?" he said.

He laughed.

Vicki jumped out of the car. "This motherfucker picked me up thinking I was a hooker! Then he recognized me and he got all embarrassed."

"It's true," Craig said. "It's all true."

I smiled and shook my head.

Vicki hugged me. Her long arms felt warm and good.

"You smell like skanky teenage girl butt," she said.

I laughed. She had a way with words.

"Did we break up?"

"Sort of."

"You still need a place to stay?"

"Yeah, just for a little while."

"You can stay with me as long as you need," she said.

Ta-Bone was giving Craig a nasty look. He was still mad about the night before.

"I saw your little fairy houses, you pussy."

Craig laughed. "You showed them Fairytown?"

I nodded.

"It's awesome, right? I built some new houses recently. For my little niece."

"Yeah, I bet," Ta-Bone said. "You love building fairy houses. Don't deny it."

"It's true," Craig said. "I can't deny it."

"I heard you guys got into a fight last night," Vicki said. "I heard you beat this old guy up really bad. I can't tell if that's sexy or sad."

Craig looked us over.

"Man," he said. "You guys really look like shit. David, do you want me to drive you to the hospital?"

"No, I'm good," I said.

"Then let me buy you guys some breakfast."

"I love breakfast," Ralph said.

"I'll fuck with some breakfast," Ta-Bone said.

As we walked toward the diner Craig put his arm around Ralph. "You can get whatever you want," he said. "Just don't jizz on me again."

"I promise."

"Ralph jizzed on our gym teacher," Ta-Bone said. "He's crazy as fuck."

"You sprayed down Mr. Phillips?"

Ralph nodded.

"That's awesome," Craig said. "Now let's go find the greasiest, most unhealthy thing on the menu and eat two orders of it."

They went inside. I stayed behind. I thought I saw something in the woods. I think it was one of the mutants. I waved to it, whatever it was, and then I went into the diner and joined my friends.

Justin Grimbol moves around a lot, and writes books. He has a medium-sized penis.

Other Grindhouse Press Titles

#666__*Satanic Summer* by Andersen Prunty

#019__*Sociopaths In Love* by Andersen Prunty

#018__*The Last Porno Theater* by Nick Cato

#017__*Zombieville* by C.V. Hunt

#016__*Samurai Vs. Robo-Dick* by Steve Lowe

#015__*The Warm Glow of Happy Homes* by Andersen Prunty

#014__*How To Kill Yourself* by C.V. Hunt

#013__*Bury the Children in the Yard: Horror Stories* by Andersen Prunty

#012 __*Return to Devil Town (Vampires in Devil Town Book Three)* by Wayne Hixon

#011__*Pray You Die Alone: Horror Stories* by Andersen Prunty

#010__*King of the Perverts* by Steve Lowe

#009__*Sunruined: Horror Stories* by Andersen Prunty

#008__*Bright Black Moon: Vampires in Devil Town Book Two* by Wayne Hixon

#007__*Hi I'm a Social Disease: Horror Stories* by Andersen Prunty

#006__*A Life On Fire* by Chris Bowsman

#005__*The Sorrow King* by Andersen Prunty

#004__*The Brothers Crunk* by William Pauley III

#003__*The Horribles* by Nathaniel Lambert

#002__*Vampires in Devil Town* by Wayne Hixon

#001__*House of Fallen Trees* by Gina Ranalli

#000__*Morning is Dead* by Andersen Prunty

www.ingramcontent.com/pod-product-compliance
Lightning Source LLC
Chambersburg PA
CBHW050421110726

47899CB00008B/2798

9780988348486